ANCESTOR'S
MAGIC

RENEE JOINER

Oshun
Publications

Book design by: Trish Beninato

www.burningphoenixcovers.com

Published by Oshun Publications

www.oshunpublications.com

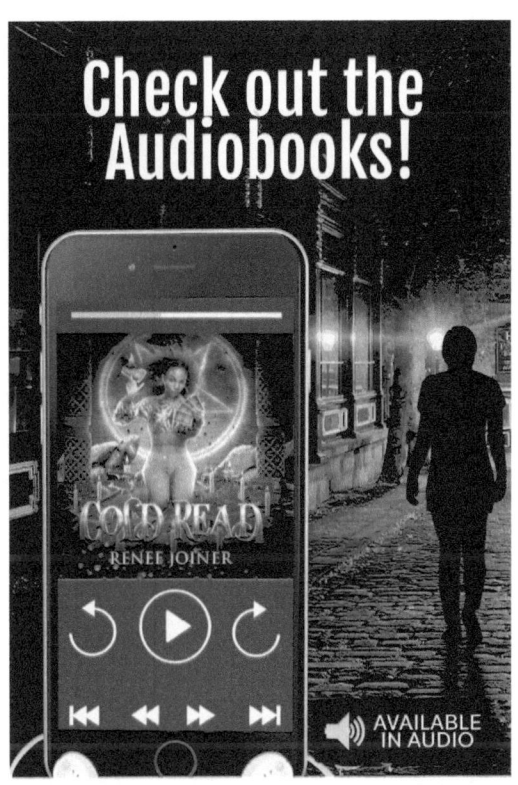

JOIN MY NEWSLETTER

GET UPDATES, FREEBIES & GIVEAWAYS

RENEEJOINERAUTHOR.COM/NEWSLETTER

SINGLES BY RENEE

Singles
Tempest
Half Demon
Wanted Undead or Alive
My Soul to Reap
Gravetide
Vance and Vance
Cold Read
Witch's Justice

ONE

ALONE IN THE DESERT

Present Day

Jade's head felt fuzzy, and her mouth was dry. She frowned as her eyes slowly opened. Her surroundings slowly came into view.

Was she still dreaming? She squeezed her eyes shut and opened them again. She wasn't dreaming! She sat up, grabbing her aching head. Where was she? She looked around, astonished to find she was in the middle of the desert. Jade's hands flew to the pockets of her jeans when she realized her phone was not with her.

Maybe it had fallen out when... She closed her eyes, trying to remember what had happened or how she'd managed to land in the desert.

Punched in the face?

The flash of memory teases her brain about some sort of scuffle, but it's gone before she can get a clear picture.

Jade pushed herself to her feet, carefully adjusting her aching head and riding out the dizziness prior to taking in the lay of the land. Looking around for her belongings, she spotted a set of tire tracks leading away from where she'd woken up. The tail end image of a scuffle teased her mind once again before leaving her frustrated with not being able to remember.

Her mouth was dry, and her stomach growled with hunger pangs. She looked up at the sky. The sun was high, which meant it was midday. Jade didn't know how long she'd been out here, but she did know that she needed to find water and shelter as soon as she could. The desert may be hot during the day, but the temperatures dropped drastically during the night. If she didn't die of heatstroke or dehydration, she very well could die of exposure.

Jade decided her best bet would be to follow the tire tracks as they should lead her out of the desert, and hopefully, she'd find something to drink along the way. Her head ached, and Jade knew it wasn't only from the scuffle but also dehydration. She needed to find water soon, or she would pass out again; only this time, she probably wouldn't wake up.

As Jade stumbled on, she was totally unaware of her bedraggled state and ignoring her injuries. Every step she took was painful, but she knew she had to push on. There was no way, after everything she'd been through in her life, she about to lay down and die now.

Men. Three? Maybe four? A wheelchair?

A ground squirrel ran across her path, and Jade sprang into action. Jade knew it may lead her to water or become a source of nourishment, so she followed it. But Jade was too weak to keep her eyes on it, and the squirrel disappeared.

Jade looked around and realized she was no longer on the tire track path. She'd been so intent on following the damn ground squirrel, she'd gotten herself lost. Her brain was still a bit foggy. She couldn't remember which way she'd come from in pursuit of the ground squirrel. As she scanned the area, an object not too far away grabbed her attention. It looked like a purse, but not just any purse—her purse.

Using what little energy she had left, Jade walked toward her purse. She dropped to her knees in front of her bag. The relief at finding it was soon overtaken by anger and frustration. The contents of her purse had been cleaned out —all her potions, powders, cards, and her orbs. There was nothing in the bag.

Anger and disappointment coursed through Jade as she flung the empty purse to the ground. What the hell was she supposed to do now? While she knelt on the hot sand, she looked around, and not too far away, she saw another familiar object. Pushing herself to her feet and scooping up her empty purse, she managed to drag herself over to it. It was her wallet. Jade reached down and picked it up. Her hands shook as she ripped it open. All her cards were still in it; even the bit of cash she'd had, but the most important thing she carried was missing.

Jade's hands shook even more as she frantically pulled the wallet apart, looking for the picture of Maya, her daughter. Why would anyone take...? The thought struck her and brought her to her knees as she buckled. She wasn't there to protect her daughter from whatever harm was on its way. And from the little Jade could piece together, and the fact that her daughter's picture was missing, harm was definitely heading Maya's way.

The combination of the baking hot sun, her injuries, and dehydration started to take its toll on Jade. She scratched through her bag and wallet once more, calling out "Maya" as she dug through it. She shoved her wallet back into her bag, yelling out her daughter's name as she did. The pain of her injuries and of not knowing what was happening to her daughter brought tears to her eyes as she started to scream Maya's name. She kept screaming her daughter's name over and over again, trying to make a connection through the Cosmos, but the connection didn't come. Her screams died down to mere whispers as her body fell over with exhaustion. The blackness reached up from within her and pulled her under.

TWO

A LITTLE BIT OF MAGIC MAKES THE BULLIES RUN AWAY

Ten Days Ago

Jade locked up the shop and headed for her car. It had been a long day, and she was looking forward to going home, ordering in, and having a movie night with her daughter, Maya. Jade started her vehicle, proceeding towards the town's small highway. As Jade turned the corner onto her street, she saw her daughter being picked on by a group of boys.

Maya tried to break through them, but they circled around her and blocked her path. Anger bubbled up inside Jade. She pulled the car over and took a few steadying breaths, calming her shaking hands, as she stepped out of her car and walked over to her daughter.

"I'm going to ask you only once to step aside and let my daughter pass." The boys turned toward Jade at the sound of her voice.

"Aww." The one boy, who was the image of his father, someone Jade had known as a bully in her youth, stepped up to her. "Little Mommy is here to turn us all into frogs," he mocked.

Jade would have loved to turn the jerk into a toad, but she refrained.

"Come on, Maya." Jade pushed juveniles aside and grabbed her daughter's hand, pulling her to the house.

"Where do you think you're going, witch?" The ringleader stepped in front of Jade, blocking her path. "That's what you are, right?" He stepped closer to Jade, pretending to be brave in front of his gang.

Jade hated the pack mentality and remembered all too well her encounters with them when she was around her daughter's age. Unfortunately, Maya was at the age when the women in Jade's family started to blossom into unrivaled beauties. This beauty tended to turn men into idiots and women into bitches. These boys were complete idiots driven by their hormones and their need to be the big dogs of the street.

"I believe I've given you fair warning." Jade's voice dropped and now held more than a hint of warning in it.

"Admit it," the boy taunted, "you're nothing but a dirty witch." He spat. "My father reckons the only good witch is a dead one." He stuck his face in Jade's.

That was it. Jade had had enough. Who the hell did this pimply, over-hormonal teenage bully think he was? Jade gave the boy a slow smile, standing her ground.

"Yes," Jade confirmed to the boy, her eyes narrowing dangerously. "I'm from an ancient coven of witches that has been around since before humans have." She told him rather smugly and enjoyed the look of confusion on his face. "I know your father," Jade told the boy. "He was a bully just like you. He tried to take my purse away one day to see what was inside it."

"Do you carry your magic wand in it?" the boy jeered, and all his friends laughed.

"After a few times of your father trying to snatch my purse, I eventually let him take it and look inside." Jade ignored the boy's sneering, and a slow smile spread across her lips. "Do you want to see what's inside my purse?" She stared directly into the boy's eyes. She could see his hesitation, but then he was pushed by his friends.

"I bet it's nothing but lady products and stale mints." He and his friends laughed again. "Or some other stinky witch stuff you carry around to fend off evil spirits coming to suck away your demon soul."

Jade flicked her hand over her purse. The latch popped open on its own, and the boys quickly took a step back. The instant two gnarled green hands with talons appeared through the opening. The boys turned and ran, screaming she was a demon and should burn in hell with Satan.

"Parlor tricks?" Maya looked at her mother, disgusted. "Really, Mom?" She shook her head and marched toward the car.

"It worked, didn't it?"

MAYA HAD DITCHED movie night as she had a big test to study for, so she went up to her room after dinner. Jade decided to go out back to her workshop and fill some of the orders she had for various herbal products. She was on her first batch of essential oils when she heard the doorbell ring in the house.

Sighing, Jade sterilized her hands and walked into the house to the front door. She wasn't surprised to see

Reverend Fletcher, the town's pastor, standing on her porch.

"Reverend Fletcher," Jade nodded to him, "what brings you to my door tonight?" She gave him a sweet smile. "Is your wife still having sleeping problems?"

"Hello Jade," the reverend greeted her. "Marjorie is sleeping well thanks to your herbs."

"I'm glad to hear that," Jade told him.

"I'm here on another matter." The reverend looked a little flushed. "I got a call this afternoon from some concerned parents who told me you were going around scaring their sons."

"Ah." Jade leaned against the doorframe and folded her arms across her chest. "Is that the story they're going with?"

"Jade, we're living on a powder keg here." The reverend took a deep breath. "You know the townsfolk are still wary of magical beings. This accord we have between you supernatural beings and us humans is a delicate one."

"Those boys had Maya cornered, and if I hadn't have come upon the scene when I had..." Jade's eyes narrowed. "All I did was an illusion to ensure they left my daughter alone."

"I understand how difficult it is for you and Maya," the reverend said sympathetically. "I'll make sure those boys are punished for their bad behavior."

"Thank you," Jade said, "but I'm afraid it will only make things worse for my daughter if you interfere."

"I understand." The revered sighed. "Rather than scaring them, come to me next time and we can defuse the situation without tricks or magic."

"What I did..." Jade defended her actions, "was nothing that went against the accord. If the accord is broken, I can assure you it won't be by me."

"That's good to know." The reverend said his good-nights and left.

"Why do you do that?" Maya asked as Jade turned around to see her standing on the stairs.

"Do what, honey?" Jade smiled at her daughter.

"Hold yourself back," Maya blurted. "You could have this whole town bowing down to you. Instead, you rein yourself in and let the humans humiliate and walk all over you."

"No one humiliates me, Maya," Jade told her daughter softly. "I stick to the accords so you can have a normal life here." She walked up to her daughter. "I've seen first-hand how quickly situations like the one you were in today can escalate."

"If I could do what you could..." Maya looked at Jade. "I wouldn't hold back." She turned and went back upstairs.

Jade sighed, staring up the stairs for a while after she heard Maya's door shut. She could remember feeling like Maya once upon a time. If truth be told, Jade had often wanted to just say to hell with it and show the humans precisely who she really was. But then she'd be no better than them with their hate and prejudices. There was a time when all creatures on Earth lived together in relative peace, or so the stories go.

Maybe one day, hopefully in the near future, that would happen again. But for now, Jade had some work to do and orders to fill. She locked the front door, made herself some herbal tea, and went back to her workshop.

THREE

THE REST STOP

Present Day

Something bumped Jade awake. Her skin felt hot and sore, her throat burned, and her head was pounding. When the stabbing pain lifted from her eyes, Jade was surprised to find herself in a car. She sat up slowly, closing her eyes for a minute as she adjusted to the light.

"You're awake!" The elderly lady in the passenger seat up front turned and smiled at her.

"How...?" Jade swallowed and gladly accepted the fresh bottle of water the lady offered her. She took a deep swallow, stopping the urge to down the whole thing in one gulp. "What happened?"

"I'm Kendal, and this here is my husband, Caleb." Kendal introduced themselves. "We were on an expedition in the desert when, to our surprise, we heard all this screaming," she explained to Jade. "So we ran toward the sound, and we saw you fall to the ground."

"I said to Kendal..." Caleb looked at Jade in the mirror, "'That young lady's in trouble.' So we got you back to our car."

"Do you have a phone?" Jade asked the couple. "I need to call home."

"I'm sorry, honey." Kendal looked at her apologetically. "But mine and Caleb's phones are dead." She held them up for Jade to see.

"Do you have a car phone charger?"

"A what?" Kendal frowned at Jade. "I didn't even know there was such a thing. Did you know about this, Caleb?"

"No." Caleb looked at Jade in the mirror. "First, I've heard of it."

"We'll be near a town soon, and you can make your call then," Kendal assured Jade. "Just sit back and relax. You've had quite the ordeal getting stranded in the desert like that."

"Do you know how long before we get there?" Jade didn't want to sound ungrateful, but she was anxious to phone Maya to find out if she was all right and to warn her.

"Here, scooch up." Kendal climbed over the front seat to hop into the back with Jade.

"Climbing over the seat like that isn't safe." Jade looked at the woman suspiciously. She was grateful to the couple for finding her, but they gave her a creepy vibe. Their concern seemed to be an illusion. Maybe it was her nerves on end.

"Oh no." Kendal laughed. "Caleb knows what he's doing on the road." She took out a first aid kit from the compartment between the seats. "Now, let me get your wounds tended to. You don't want to scar such pretty skin."

"Thank you." Jade flinched a little as Kendal cleaned her cuts.

"You must be starving," Kendal said and pulled a sandwich out of a cooler bag on the floor next to her. "Here you go."

"That looks delicious," Jade said realizing how hungry she was and bit into the sandwich.

While she ate, Kendal finished tending to Jade's wounds. The couple hadn't asked her any questions about how or why she was in the desert. Jade wanted to believe they were giving her time to recuperate or didn't want to offend her, but she was still wary of them.

"There's a petrol station just up ahead," Caleb told her. "We're going to stop for gas if you need to use the restrooms."

"That sounds good." Jade felt relief flood through her. Maybe they would have a phone she could use.

A few minutes later, Caleb pulled onto a side road, deserted with the exception of a lone gas station. Jade looked out of the window. The gas station looked like something out of a horror movie. Years of ivy grew on the building as well as every available post. There were only two pumps and a pink sign in the small store window that flashed *open*. Another sign on the doors read *fresh pies made daily onsite*. Jade shuddered, wondering about what the kitchen those pies were made in looked like.

Jade climbed out of the car, grabbed her bag, and walked into the store. As expected, a little bell tinkled from above. The store was surprisingly clean, with neat shelves that were well stocked. Still, Jade couldn't shake the creepy feeling the place gave her. Everything was not as it seemed.

"Can I help you, Miss?" a male voice asked, making Jade jump.

Jade turned towards the checkout counter where a young man stood, staring at her as if she was a piece of candy. Slowly, and with a bit of apprehension, Jade walked over to the counter.

"Do you have a phone I can borrow?" Jade asked him.

"I do," the young man told her, "but we don't get much signal around here, so I'm afraid your call may not go through." He handed Jade his phone.

Thanking him, Jade took it, looking for the best place in the store to find a signal. Once she had a few bars in a spot near the rear windows of the shop, she dialed Maya's number. The call went through, but there was no answer. Jade tried another three times, each time leaving her daughter a message to be careful and that she'd be home soon.

Frustration bubbled in Jade when she lost the signal just before she decided to try again. She walked back to the store clerk and gave him back his phone.

"Is there a restroom I can use?" Jade asked him.

"Yeah." The young man handed her the key. "It's through the back there."

Jade took the key and walked off to the restroom. It wasn't hard to find, and once again, she was pleasantly surprised at how clean it was. She turned to the mirror and was shocked by what she saw. There were pieces of foliage in her hair, and her face was smeared with dirt. Her clothes were filthy. It was bad; she could smell her own pit sweat.

Jade went to the toilet, and when she was finished, she washed her hands and then went to work using a paper towel to give herself a quick wash, including her underarms. She wondered if Kendal would have some deodorant. A cold shiver tickled her spine when she thought about the couple waiting for her outside. Something about them was not quite right.

Images of a struggle once again flashed through Jade's mind. Suddenly thoughts went to Maya. She needed to get back to town in a hurry. Every instinct in Jade's body screamed that Maya was in trouble—the kind of trouble

Jade knew only she could help with. For the first time in a long time, Jade thought about her own mother, and she wished she were back home.

Tears sprung to Jade's eyes as the past few days' stress, anger, and trauma started to take their toll on her. She looked in her purse, pulling out her wallet, before turning it over to give it a shake. Nothing! Her frustration grew inside her, as did the fear for her daughter's life. She had to do something.

In her mind's eye, Jade saw the ground squirrel she was chasing. The ground squirrel was not only to be a source of food for Jade. She looked around the restroom for something sharp. She could break a mirror, but that would attract attention to herself. Right now, she needed time to prepare and draw on her strength.

FOUR

A SICK FAMILY WITH AN EVIL AGENDA

Exhausted and upset, Jade turned her wrist over to the soft underside. This was going to hurt, but what was a little pain compared to saving her daughter's life? Jade had just started scratching on her skin with her nails, trying to draw blood, when the door to the restroom burst open.

The shop attendant stared at her with an appalling look that Jade had seen once before in his eyes, but the memory of it was just out of reach. She dropped her arm but carried on scratching into the skin as she stared at the shop attendant.

"I don't think you're allowed to be in here." Jade used her shoulder to wipe a tear from her cheek.

The young man didn't say a word. Instead, he kicked the door shut while continuing to stare at her. Jade stopped scratching her skin and rinsed off her hands before trying to step around the man, but he stepped in front of her, blocking her way while leering down at her.

Jade's heart started to beat in her chest as flashes from a similar scene when she was young played through her mind. His pupils dilated as he looked at her like she was his prey.

"Please move out of my way," Jade told him, her eyes narrowing, and she stood defiantly looking up at him.

The reek of his foul breath and body odor filled the space between them, making her want to wretch. The man wouldn't move from Jade's path, instead he stepped closer to her, grabbing her wrist.

"Let me go!" Jade fought to free her wrist from his grasp, but he grabbed her other one and pushed her back against the bathroom wall. "No!" She struggled against him and soon realized that the more she fought, the more aroused he was getting. "Stop this!" Her throat ached as she screamed for help, but no one could hear her.

The young man secured both her wrists above her head with one hand while he started to pull off his pants with the other. Jade saw a gap and managed to raise her leg enough to kick him in the knee as hard as she could. His shocked gaze locked with her frightened one. His grip on her wrists slackened. Jade took full advantage of it, kicking him again in the same knee, making the young man buckle in pain. When he grabbed his knee, Jade ripped her hands free of his sweaty ones. Before he could recapture her, she punched him as hard as she could in the solar plexus, knocking the breath from him.

Jade managed to grab her empty bag while dashing from the restroom, screaming for help. She ran straight for the shop door, where she saw Caleb reaching out to open it.

"That man attacked me!" Jade's eyes were filled with shock and fear. She hurtled through the door and into Caleb's arms.

Before she knew what was happening, Caleb's arms tightened around her, locking her against him.

"What?" Jade looked up at Caleb in confusion when he pulled her closer, cupping her buttocks with his hand.

"Relax, darlin'," Caleb sneered into her ear. "We're just going to have a little fun until our customers arrive. They want to have little fun with you too." His hot breath blew in her ear. "God, I wish I could throw you down right here and mount you hard and rough." He laughed as he felt Jade struggling to break free of his bear-like hold. "Oh, honey. That just makes me want you so much more."

"Let me go!" Jade tried to push herself free, but he'd grabbed hold of her hands.

"Here comes the missus." Caleb cleared his throat and sighed. "Pity we have to let Junior break you in." He spun her around to face Kendal while keeping her locked in his arms.

"Come here, you little bitch." Kendal walked toward Jade with a cable tie in her hands.

"She's a real hot one, this one." Caleb rubbed himself suggestively against Jade's bottom. "I can't wait to take her for a ride."

"Relax, Papa," Kendal snapped at him as he forced Jade's hands together in front of her so that Kendal could secure them with the cable tie. "Junior needs to become a man, and today's that day. We can have our fun with her when he's done." She ran her dirty finger down Jade's throat and between her breasts. "Don't go getting ideas now, as I don't want to lose money having to slit your pretty little throat." She leaned in, getting close to Jade's face, and whispered, "Don't go...."

Jade's chest rose and fell as Kendal dragged her into the shop and threw her on the floor near the fridges. She tried to push herself up, but Kendal's booted foot pushed her back down into a lying position on the floor.

"Junior!" Kendal yelled, "come on, boy. She's ready for ya." Kendal straddled Jade and started to push her top up, her eyes filling with desire. "You should be grateful to us. We could've let you die in the desert and be eaten by wild animals." She started to unbutton Jade's pants. "Now be good to my boy and show him what whores like you are for."

"I'm ready, Momma." Junior had recovered from his spat with Jade in the bathroom and now stood above her, pulling down his pants. "I want to finish ripping off her clothes." His eyes were wild with excitement, and his manhood was straining against his underpants.

Kendal repositioned herself. Standing above her, she pulled Jade's arms above her head.

"Lie still, you dirty whore," Kendal warned Jade.

Her shock had started to wear off, and the fear that had paralyzed her as the scene in front of her unfolded brought back painful memories that disappeared the moment Junior knelt over her and started to force his hand into her waistband.

"No!" Jade started to struggle.

This was not going to happen to her again. She was older and stronger now.

"Lie still, bitch." Kicking Jade in the head, Kendal tried to subdue her.

Jade bucked her hips and dislodged Junior. As he knelt over her again, Jade twisted and kicked wildly. Junior grabbed her legs and started to pull down her pants. He looked even more excited. Before her waistband cleared her hips, Jade closed her eyes and breathed. The world around her started to pulse as she drew energy from the Earth to fuel her power.

"Wake up!" Kendal slapped Jade's cheeks. Her eyes flew open, and she looked up at Kendal, who drew back in fright. Jade knew her eyes had changed color. She could feel her powers igniting as the bottles started to rattle and explode in the fridge.

"What the hell?" Junior jumped off Jade and ducked as goods from the shelf were hurled at him.

"Stop this!" Kendal yanked on Jade's wrists, but the ties snapped, freeing Jade's hands.

As Jade sat up, Kendal sprung at her, but Jade raised her hand, and Kendal was suddenly pinned against the cold door of the refrigerator. Jade stood up, her hair rising as a kinetic force swirled around her. Junior ran at her, screaming for her to let his mother go. Jade turned to look at him. Her violet eyes were blank as a smile lifted one side of her mouth. She sent him flying through the glass door of one of the refrigerators.

She turned as Caleb came up behind her, swinging a spade at her head. Jade held up her hand, and the spade was yanked from Caleb's hand, landing in Jade's.

"Thanks for the lift," Jade said to Caleb before she swung the spade with all her might and connected it with Caleb's head.

Caleb's face moved with the spade. His eyes were huge with shock before he crumpled to the ground. Jade bent down, searching through Caleb's pockets for his car keys. She dumped the spade next to Caleb's unconscious body. Jade stood up, walked to the counter, grabbed some red licorice, and picked up her purse that she'd dropped near the door. Before she left the shop, she looked down at the scratches on her arm. Pictures of her chasing the ground squirrel ran across her mind once again. Food was not the only reason she'd needed that ground squirrel.

Jade turned back to see Junior pulling himself out of the fridge. He was bleeding and unsteady on his feet, but he pushed himself toward his mother. Kendal was still held by a telekinetic force that stuck her to the cold door like a giant magnet. Jade ignored Junior and Kendal's rants as she made her way toward them, stopping near the broken fridge door. She tilted her head to look down at the floor. Jade could feel it.

Things had changed. The balance had been shifted. Jade could feel it. She'd felt it moments before she'd met the man who'd betrayed her. When he'd taken away her orbs and herbs, leaving her to die in the desert, he'd broken the tight restrictions that bound her to specific human rules. Rules that she was forced to adhere to so she could live at peace in her hometown.

But Jade had never really known peace anywhere. Like the rest of her kind, she'd been treated differently and, at times, with extreme prejudice. She'd been ridiculed, sexually assaulted twice now, but she was not allowed to defend herself. She wasn't the villain here, and neither was she back then. The power that Jade could feel flowing through her was not even a fraction of the power she kept contained and hidden deep within her. Her power had been shackled for far too long. Jade had lived up to her end of the accords, but the humans were yet to live up to theirs. This latest incident was an act of war.

Seeing her staring at the floor, Junior ran at Jade once again.

"Let my mother go, you crone of a whore!" Junior's face turned red with anger as he hurtled toward her. "I'll burn you on a pyre, like all you devil's spawn should be."

Jade lifted her head toward the young man dragging his badly bleeding leg toward her. She stared at him for a minute. Images of him attacking her in the restroom and on the floor were fresh in her mind. Before Junior could get too close to her, she raised her hand, balled her fist, and twisted. Junior grasped his neck and dropped to his knees, gasping for breath.

"Let my boy go!" Kendal shouted at Jade. "Let him go!"

Jade bent down and picked up a shard of glass from the floor in front of the refrigerator. She held the fragment in her hand, examining the sharp object. Jade came from one of the oldest witch lines, powerful ancient magic ran through her veins while her ancestors waited beyond the veil for her to tap into their resources to add to her power.

"My baby!" Kendal's screams had Jade turning toward the woman.

"I should let you all rot in hell," Jade told Kendal while running her finger over the glass shard. "But you're going to get what's coming to you." She smiled, touching her finger to the tip of the glass, and drawing a drop of blood. "I'd stay to watch, but I've something to attend to." Jade drew a symbol on the third fridge door with her blood. "You and your sick family have been marked." Her eyes glinted when they looked at Kendal.

When she got to the front door, she turned to face Kendal and Junior once again.

"Thanks for the loan of your car." Jade held up Caleb's car keys. "I'll take good care of it." She flicked her wrist, and Junior fell forward gasping for air as soon as the invisible band around his throat disappeared. The young man wasn't about to let her go, and he sprang to his feet and tried to run at Jade, sore leg and all.

"Junior, no!" Kendal screamed at her son.

Junior had not taken more than a few steps when he was flung back against a shelf and crumpled unconscious to the floor.

"I'll get you for this!" Kendal screamed after Jade as she

left the shop carrying a shard of glass, a bottle of water, and some red licorice. "You bloody witch! I'll find you!" The door banged shut, drowning out Kendal's threats.

FIVE

A DAY LIKE ANY OTHER

Eight Days Ago

Jade had just walked in from working in her herb work-shop when she saw a car pull up in front of the house. Grabbing a cloth to wipe her hands, she walked toward the window as Maya got out of the car and then leaned back in to kiss the boy in the driver's seat. Jade couldn't believe what she'd just seen. Maya hadn't told her she was seeing a boy.

The front door opened as the car sped off. Jade said a silent incantation, and the car slowed down to a safer speed. She smiled. The boy would not be driving over the speed limit any time soon. She felt a little bad using magic on the boy, but she'd just done their community a favor, as that driver was reckless.

"Mom!" Maya stopped at the door when she saw Jade staring at her. "I didn't know you'd be home."

"Obviously." Jade folded her arms. "Who's your friend?" she asked.

"No one to concern yourself about," Maya told her and headed for her bedroom, slamming the door.

Jade sighed and shook her head. Why couldn't they stay little, happy, and obedient forever? She walked into the kitchen to make Maya a snack and pour her some juice. Maybe with something in her stomach, Maya would be more cooperative. Jade put a few cookies on the plate to sweeten her daughter up a bit.

As she walked up the stairs and drew nearer to Maya's room, she heard her talking to someone, and a distinct smell of weed drifted to her.

"What the hell!" Jade stormed up to Maya's bedroom door and shoved it open without knocking.

There was a big scramble as the boy she was sure was driving the car jumped off the bed, grabbed the bong, and dove out of Maya's window.

"Mom!" Maya screamed at her mother. "How dare you barge into my room!"

"You've got a boy up here smoking pot?" Jade's temper snapped as she yelled at Maya. "What is going on with you?"

"Stop trying to control my life!" Maya's fist balled at her side as she faced Jade. "I'm not a screw-up like you. I've got my life under control."

"Really?" Jade screamed back. "Smoking pot and sneaking boys into your room is under control?"

"If I told you my friend wanted to come over, you would've said no!" Maya yelled.

"We'll never know now, will we?" Jade retorted, pushing past her daughter to walk over and lock the window magically before collecting Maya's electronics. "I want your homework done in two hours, and you won't be seeing these for devices for two weeks."

"You bitch." Maya tried to take the phone and tablet back from Jade. "Give them back."

"No." Jade held on to the devices. "And you're grounded for two months. You will go to school on the bus, and you will come home on the bus." Her eyes narrowed warningly. "Don't defy me on this, or think I won't know if you try to sneak around with that boy or smoke pot again."

"Really?" Maya's eyes glittered with anger. "And what are you going to do if I disobey? Burn down the town again?"

Jade went deathly still, and before she could stop herself, her hand flew out, connecting with Maya's cheek.

"Get out!" Maya's eyes filled with tears as she looked at Jade in shock. "I hate you." She pushed Jade out of her bedroom door and locked it behind her.

The anger that burned through Jade made her shake. She stood hugging Maya's devices while staring at the locked bedroom door. Jade needed to cool down. She needed to get out of the house and head down to see Suzie, her one friend at the town bar.

Jade hid Maya's electronics, grabbed her car keys, and picked up her purse before heading out the door. Before she left, she cast a spell upon the house—no one in, no one out, except for her. Jade hated magically locking her daughter in the house, but she was safe, and Jade knew she wouldn't be able to leave the house to do something stupid. Jade had been fifteen once and knew what that kind of stupid could look like.

SUZIE POURED Jade a shot to cool her down and put a bottle of beer in front of her.

"This will take the edge off." Suzie smiled at Jade. "We

were once Maya's age," she reminded Jade before going off to serve a customer.

Jade opened her wallet and swallowed down the shot before staring at the picture of her Maya. How she wished their lives were simpler. She knew it wasn't easy for her. This was the year her powers would start to fully manifest, which Jade had never thought was fair. You had enough hormones and other changes to cope with during your teen years without adding magical changes to the list.

Jade took a sip of her beer while running her finger over the picture of her daughter. Her mind drifted back to when she was Maya's age and started to date a normal human boy. Jade's mother, Grace Lawrence, was so good about it. She supported Jade, and they had an open mother/daughter relationship, until one night Jade had stayed out two hours over her curfew.

She sighed and took another sip. That night had produced a fight with her mother just as bad, if not worse, than Jade's fight with Maya a little while ago. When Jade had gotten home and tried to sneak into the house, Grace had been waiting for her. Initially, Grace had just been worried and warned Jade about staying out late. She'd told Jade there were evil people in this world, and they especially liked to lurk about at night.

"Can I buy you another beer?" a deep voice asked her, jolting her back to reality.

Jade turned to see a tall, handsome man with sandy brown hair and hazel eyes smiling down at her.

"I'm fine, thank you," Jade told him, a little coldly.

She had mixed feelings about him, but then again, it could just be the shot clouding her judgment, although alcohol didn't affect her as it did normal people. Regardless, she was in no mood for company. She'd never seen him before. He was obviously not from around here, as Jade knew every face in this small town.

"I'm Dave," he told her. "Mind if I sit here?" He pointed to the empty barstool next to Jade.

"It's not my seat." Jade gave him a tight smile before closing her wallet and putting it back into her purse.

Jade downed the rest of her beer and said goodnight to Suzie as she picked up her purse and left the bar. She never gave Dave another glance or saw the way his eyes narrowed while watching her leave the bar.

"MAYA?" Jade knocked on her daughter's bedroom door. "Can I come in?"

"Even if I said no, you would anyway," Maya called from the other side of the door.

Jade sighed and rested her head against the door before opening it. She didn't walk into the room. Instead, Jade stood at the door and watched her daughter doing her homework at her desk.

"Do you need any help?" Jade asked. "I have some snacks." She walked over to the desk and put down the plate of food she'd prepared for Maya.

"Thanks," Maya said, ignoring Jade and carrying on with her work.

"I'm sorry. I shouldn't have lashed out like that. I know what it's like to be fifteen and from a line of witches." Jade smiled as Maya turned her chair around to look at her.

"I'm sorry too," Maya apologized. "I just wanted to fit in, and I really like Wade," she told Jade honestly.

"I promise to try and be more understanding and less controlling." Jade raised her eyebrows. "If you promise to always be open and honest with me." She took Maya's hands in hers. "But we have to have some ground rules."

"Okay." Maya's brows drew together.

"No more drugs, and that includes any form of pot," Jade said to Maya.

"That was my first time," Maya told her mother, her cheeks turning pink. "I didn't like the smell, taste, or the fuzzy feeling."

"Good." Jade smiled. "I want to know when Wade is bringing you home, and ask if he can come here instead of him sneaking in."

After they'd cleared the air and set the ground rules, Jade unsealed Maya's bedroom window and gave back her devices. However, Maya was still grounded for two weeks and had to increase her chores for the weeks while she was grounded.

That night, when Jade locked up, she felt good about her talk and relationship with Maya, but there was something else in the air that sent a chill up her spine that she could not quite put her finger on. She shivered, chalking it up to her awful fight with Maya as she climbed the stairs to her bedroom.

SIX

A NIGHT OUT

Six Days Ago

Jade looked at her watch as she jogged down the street. She liked this time of the morning to jog as all the other joggers had already run and were now at work. As she came up to the local supermarket, Jade saw an elderly woman coming out of the store carrying some heavy grocery bags. She was going to run and ask the woman if she could help her when a tall, handsome, familiar man walked out and took the bags from her.

It was Dave, the man who had tried to buy Jade a drink at the bar the other night. He looked up as he and the woman walked her way. His face lit up in a look of pleasant surprise.

"Hi." Dave greeted her as he and the lady came upon her.

"Hi." Jade smiled at him before greeting the woman walking with him.

"How are you?" Dave smiled.

"I'm good, thank you." Jade looked at her watch. She had to get the store open. "Excuse me. I have somewhere to be," she said before saying goodbye and jogging away. Well, that was awkward, Jade thought, as she finished her run and did a cool-down on her porch.

As she showered, she thought about Dave. He seemed to be quite a nice guy helping out an elderly lady. Jade would meet Suzie at the bar later, so maybe Dave would be there again tonight. She dried off and went to open her shop. Jade still wasn't able to shake the feeling from the night of her big fight with Maya.

The day was pretty uneventful as Jade delivered tinctures, creams, and other herbal items to her regular customer and the shops that stocked her products. She was on the way to make her deliveries when her friend Suzie sent her a message reminding her of their night out. Jade messaged her back, telling her she'd be there on time this time. But as long as they have known each other, Jade has always been late.

When she got home, Maya was getting ready to go to the movies with her friend and the boy she was seeing. Maya had agreed that Jade could cast a spell on her as a precaution in case anything happened. Maya was going on her first movie date with a normal boy. Jade still had emotional scars from her teenage years, and she would be damned if she'd let anything happen to Maya. Jade knew just how vicious teenagers could be, especially to their kind. They were bound by an accord that her kind, especially Jade, could not use her magic; well, not in public anyway, or on another person. Her daughter wasn't just any person, and she was an easy target for stupid teenagers, like the boys who had been messing with Maya the other day.

"Mom?" Maya walked into the kitchen where Jade was putting away the leftover salad from their dinner.

"You look nice." Jade looked at Maya's jeans, pink shirt,

and matching pink sneakers. "Do you have a jacket?"

"Yes." Maya pointed to a denim jacket she'd thrown over the back of an armchair, her purse sitting on top of it.

"Hold on." Jade closed the refrigerator and then hurried to her purse on the table by the front door. She fiddled inside and pulled out her wallet. "Here you go." She gave Maya some money. "You may need an Uber or something?"

"Thanks, Mom." Maya gave Jade a hug as a car pulled up in front of the house. "He's here."

"Wait for him to come to the door," Jade told her excited daughter. "I would like to meet him."

The doorbell rang. Jade told Maya to get her jacket while she answered the door.

"Hello." Jade looked at the tall young man who was appeared nervous. "Can I help you?"

"Um, hi." The young man gave Jade a big smile as he cleared this throat. "I'm Wade."

"Hello, Wade." Jade looked him in the eyes as if she was trying to read him. "I hope you don't intend to drink, smoke, or do any form of recreational drugs while taking my daughter out."

"MOM!" Maya ran up to the door, trying to push Jade out of the way, but Jade stood her ground.

"It's okay, Maya." Wade gave Maya a warm smile. "Your mother has every right to question me that."

"Well?" Jade folded her arms across her chest. She would not fall for the 'butter up the girlfriend's mother' routine.

"No," Wade said honestly. "I am not on, nor do I intend to take, any recreational drugs, and I don't drink alcohol."

"Fine." Jade's eyes narrowed. "But I will know if you do." She gave Wade a big smile. "Now, go enjoy your night."

Maya shook her head at Jade and rolled her eyes before

giving Jade a hug and then rushing out the door before her mother could embarrass her again.

Jade watched Maya and Wade get into the car and drive away. She closed the front door. Her eye caught the time on the giant clock that hung on the living room wall. She needed to go get ready. She was meeting Suzie in thirty minutes.

THE BAR WAS BUSTLING. There were a lot of people from out of town for some convention or other. Suzie had organized a band to play for the next few nights, so many of the locals had dusted off their dancing shoes to have a fun evening out.

"It's an excellent number of people here for the bar, Suzie." Jade sipped her white wine.

"I know." Suzie held up her glass of wine in salute. "I needed this kind of crowd."

"If you get a local band in on the weekends, you'd be bound to have an attendance like this." Jade laughed as they watched couples twirling around the makeshift dance floor. "The local folk love having a good night on the town."

"If I have a few more nights like this one," Suzie said, taking a sip of her crisp white wine, "I'll be able to afford one."

"I'm a little mad that you said you'd take a late shift." Jade narrowed her eyes as she looked at Suzie. "I was looking forward to us having a full night out."

"Yeah, right." Suzie grinned at Jade. "You're going to want to be home by eleven to make sure Maya comes home."

"As usual..." Jade lifted her drink toward Suzie. "You

are correct."

"Hell, if you didn't, I would race to your house to make sure she was home at eleven." Suzie's eyebrows lifted. "This must've been how our mothers felt at our age."

"I feel for parents of normal, non-magical kids." Jade sighed. "They have no way of protecting their kids like we do."

"In a way, I'm glad I have a boy." Suzie took a long swallow of her wine. "They don't come into their magic until they're in their early twenties."

"You're also lucky because you grew up in this town with your father," Jade said softly. "No one knows about you."

"Every day, I'm thankful to your mother for that," Suzie breathed. "I don't know how my father would've coped when we came to this town if it weren't for the help of your mom."

"Hell, Suzie, you and your dad took me in when my mom left," Jade reminded Suzie. "Thanks to your hunky warlock husband, when Jack's powers do come to him, it will be accredited to Ethan's side of the family and not yours."

"Until Jack exhibits extraordinary powers, I'm not looking forward to ever having to explain that."

"You won't have to if you teach Jack how to control them." Jade leaned forward on the table, twirling the stem of her wine glass.

"Thanks to your mother binding my magic," Suzie refilled their glasses with the bottle of wine they had on ice, "I have no powers. I'm hoping that maybe I didn't pass any of my magical lines on to Jack."

"You know it doesn't work that way, right?" Jade shook her head.

"I can hope." Suzie shrugged, lifting her glass.

"If it were that easy, I would've had my powers bound, and then Maya wouldn't have to go through all the shit we had to at her age." Jade sighed.

"I didn't go through it as badly as you did." Suzie covered Jade's hand with hers. "I hated seeing the way you suffered through your teens. You should've been allowed to go into the woods that border the town and let your powers blossom like they needed to."

"I managed." Jade gave Suzie a small smile. "And that was thanks to you."

"Yeah, our little road trips into the desert!" Suzie winked at Jade.

"If it weren't for those trips, I probably would've exploded long before the incident." Jade's face dropped.

"Hey!" Suzie looked past Jade. "Isn't that the handsome stranger who tried to buy you a drink the other night?"

Jade felt her heart skip a beat as she turned at the same time Dave did. Their eyes met and held. He nodded as a way of greeting before turning back toward the bar and perching himself on a barstool.

"Suzie?" A waitress came over to Jade and Suzie's table. "I know you're not officially working tonight, but we could really use your help behind the bar. The new guy isn't keeping up too well."

Suzie and Jade turned to see Ethan, Suzie's husband, being run ragged behind the bar.

"Talking about magically exploding..." Jade grinned at Ethan as he looked their way. "I think your husband needs you."

"He wanted to be more involved in the bar since he had to quit the army." Suzie shrugged. "So I let him start behind the bar."

"He was injured, Suzie." Jade shook her head at her friend. "You know he's not allowed to magically heal himself."

"If this town stopped their shit..." Suzie downed the last of her wine. "We'd all be able to help heal everyone." She picked up her purse, empty wine glass, and bottle. "Why don't you come and join me at the bar?" She gave Jade a wicked grin. "There's a barstool with your name on it next to the tall, dark, handsome stranger."

"Well, that was subtle..." Jade shook her head. "But I should go and apologize for my bad behavior the other night."

"Yes, you should." Suzie nodded and grinned as she walked off.

Jade downed the last of her wine, picked up her purse, jacket, and glass before making her way to the bar.

"Hi," Jade said as she put her things down on the bar next to Dave. "Mind if I sit here?"

"It's not my stool." Dave turned toward her and smiled.

"Touché." Jade nodded and sat down. Suzie appeared and took Jade's purse and jacket to put behind the bar before filling up her glass with wine. "Thanks." Jade smiled at Suzie.

"It's nice to know the owner." Dave gave Jade a small smile. "I had to wait quite a while to be served."

"You're not as pretty as her." Ethan put another beer in front of Dave. "On the house for your long wait to be served." He turned and walked away.

"Thanks," Dave said to Ethan's back. "He's quite the mountain, isn't he?" Dave referred to Ethan's six-foot-five frame.

"He is..." Jade took a sip of her wine. "But his heart is just as big as he is."

"Good to know." Dave nodded.

"I just wanted to apologize for how rude I was to you the other night," Jade said to Dave. "It was wrong of me to take my personal baggage out on a complete stranger."

"Ah." Dave turned toward Jade. "Let me guess... You wanted to go out after your curfew, but your overprotective mother wouldn't let you."

"How did you guess?" Jade laughed.

For the next two hours, Jade and Dave chatted. Jade told Dave how she had married her childhood sweetheart, and they had a child together, but their marriage wasn't built to last. Her ex-husband couldn't take the stress of married life or being a father.

Dave told Jade that he wasn't in town for long. He came to town to do a job for his older brother. After a few beers, Dave opened up to Jade and told her he didn't think he could ever live up to his older brother's achievements.

Dave showed Jade a signet ring that Jade told him looked just like the one Reverend Fletcher had and joked about them being in a secret society. When Dave explained the ring belonged to his late father and how he didn't think he had deserved or earned the ring, Jade felt bad for joking about it.

Jade's phone alarm went off. It was 10:30, time for her to head home. Dave offered to give her a lift home, and she accepted. It was better than taking an Uber which she couldn't pay for.

They pulled up outside Jade's house.

"Dave..." Jade looked at his ring. "If your brother is so accomplished, why doesn't he have the ring and whatever mantle comes with it?"

"It's complicated." Dave sighed and gave her a sexy smile.

"I can understand that." Jade smiled back at him and got out of the car.

Dave jumped out as well and followed Jade to her door.

"I had a great time tonight," Dave said softly, as his voice became husky.

"I did too." Jade's pupils dilated as their eyes locked.

Dave and Jade stepped together; his arms snaked around her and pulled her close to his body as his lips came down on hers. There was instant desire as Jade pressed her body against his while wrapping her arms around his neck. She could feel his passion rise as her body melted against his.

The front door flew open, making Dave and Jade jump apart.

"Hello, Mom." Maya gave Jade a knowing look.

Jade's cheeks were flushed with passion, and her chest still rose and fell from the intensity of it. She'd felt an attraction to Dave on the first night they'd met, but she'd never expected it to be this consuming.

"Maya!" Jade looked at her wristwatch. "You're home 10 minutes early."

"I got home 10 minutes ago." Maya tapped her foot. "Check your phone. I sent you a message and a picture with the house in the background for proof."

"Maya, this is Dave." Jade introduced them. "Dave, this is my daughter, Maya."

"Hi, want to come in for coffee?" she asked Dave, who accepted.

Twenty minutes later, Maya went to bed, leaving Dave and Jade alone in the living room.

"She's a great kid." Dave smiled at Jade, his eyes darkening with passion as he moved closer to Jade on the sofa.

"She is." Jade gave Dave a seductive smile and moved closer to Dave.

Dave pulled Jade into his arms and kissed her. Jade straddled Dave's lap. Dave placed his hands on Jade's buttocks and slid her close to him. Their kiss intensified as need built up in Jade. It had been a long time since she'd had a lover. She knew she had to have him but didn't want Maya catching them.

Jade stopped the kiss to stare into Dave's passion-filled eyes. She gave him a slow, seductive smile before getting off his lap and pulling him up to drag him out the back door and into her workhouse.

As she pushed the door closed, Dave pulled her back toward him to crush her lips to his once again. His hands were all over her body, pulling her clothes off while she went to work on his clothes. His body was magnificent. Jade wanted to kiss every inch of it. When they were naked, Jade pushed Dave onto the sofa where he pulled her on top of him.

THAT NIGHT, at the other end of town, Reverend Fletcher received a disturbing call. The caller would not identify themself but demanded the reverend tell them the terms of the accord. The reverend wanted to know why, but the caller would not say.

"Look, I don't know what you're thinking of doing or what this is all about," Reverend Fletcher spoke into the receiver of his phone, "but this is a peaceful town. No normal person or witch can be harmed in this town. Is that clear?"

The caller said nothing before the line went dead.

SEVEN

THE LAST SERMON OF REVEREND FLETCHER

Present Day

Jade parked Caleb's car at the edge of the town near Reverend Fletcher' house. Her panic and fear at being violated by that foul family had awakened Jade's long-dormant power. It was a power that was just blossoming before it was extinguished all those years ago when her mother had signed the accords that stunted Jade's magical growth. Now that power was free, and instead of it slowly growing as Jade grew, it was now bursting out all at once.

Jade could feel its glorious warmth as it filled that hole inside of her that always made her feel like something was missing in her life. It was a hole that she'd tried to fill with love, motherhood, and healing, or bringing relief and joy to others through her healing herbs, while using parlor tricks and soft magic behind closed doors to keep her skills sharp. But she still always felt so empty. The only joy she had was her daughter—a daughter she couldn't get a hold of and who was not at home.

Jade had called all of Maya's friends when she'd come home. No one—not even Wade, who'd left about 8o messages on Jade's phone—knew where she was. When she'd called Wade back, the boy seemed genuinely concerned and hadn't seen Maya since he'd dropped her off at home the afternoon before. Jade needed to do a locator spell to find her daughter, but she knew that would draw power and attention to herself. So, before turning the town upside down, she would pay the good Reverend Fletcher a visit.

Light glinted from the ground, momentarily blinded her. A message from her ancestors? A triumphant smile lifted Jade's face as she picked up the shard of glass. Holding it tightly in her hand, she knew her own blood was more powerful than any others and drew a more profound, much older magic to her. With the herbs she always carried, Jade mixed them with an ancient pestle left to her by her ancestors in her family's sacred mortar. She sliced her palm with the glass shard she'd collected from the place where her magic had reappeared and dropped her blood into the bowl while she chanted.

Within seconds, her ancestors answered her. A swirl of magic rose up and twirled around her form. She breathed in the power, closing her eyes and throwing her arms open wide to embrace it and let it into her soul.

The magic entered her body with a force that almost overwhelmed her. Once she'd absorbed it all, she fell to the floor exhausted and lay there for a few minutes as her body adjusted to its new dynamic. As her breathing slowed and her heart rate decreased, energy started to flow through her again. She pushed herself to her feet. She felt so alive and whole. She also no longer felt so alone as she drove to the good Reverend Fletcher's.

It was a short ride with Jade climbing out of the car before it came to a dead stop. She didn't bother to take the keys. It wasn't her car, after all. She started to walk a few feet to the reverend's house. With every step she took, her anger, panic, and fear for her daughter fueled her power. By the time she'd gotten to the reverend's front door, her hair had flown out behind her, and her eyes were a violet color as the magic flowed through her.

Jade didn't bother to knock. With a slight movement of her head, the door burst open and hung half off its hinges. Hearing the bang, the reverend and his family had rushed into the hallway. Reverend Fletcher's eyes grew wide when he saw the state of Jade. She hadn't bothered to change her filthy clothes she'd been left in the desert with. The reverend stepped protectively in front of his family, telling them to run, but they couldn't move.

"Jade," the reverend said calmly, "what are you doing?"

"Funny thing," Jade said, stepping uninvited over the threshold. As she did, the wind, caused by her power, made the pictures fly off the wall in all directions, including toward the reverend that lifted both arms to fend the objects off. "I was attacked and left in the desert to die." She stopped and stared at the reverend and his terrified family.

"What?" The reverend's brows creased together. "My family had nothing to do with that, Jade. If you just calm down, we can talk about it, and I will find out why that happened or who did it."

"Come now, reverend..." Jade tilted her head to look at him. "You know exactly why."

"Well, Jade, if this is the way you react to what I could only imagine being a childish prank or retaliation for scaring those boys the other day..." Reverend Fletcher' voice became stern, "Can you blame them for not wanting a witch around?"

"You know, we were in his town long before any of you

humans were." Jade used to think she, too, was human, only with a special gift.

But she soon realized humans were nothing like magical beings. They were vicious, greedy, selfish, and cold-blooded monsters, yet they feared magical creatures who had protected and nurtured humans since their time began.

"You know we don't believe that, Jade." Reverend Fletcher tried to back up as Jade took another step closer, but he couldn't move. "If you calm down, I'll forgive this little outburst. We can talk this out and sort out what happened to you."

"Where's my daughter?" Jade's eyes narrowed at the reverend.

"I have no idea." Reverend Fletcher swallowed. "Have you tried your house?"

"No," Jade said sarcastically, "I never thought to go look there first or call all her friends and teachers, and—"

"Okay, I get it." Reverend Fletcher nodded. "I'll help you find her if you calm down." He lifted his hand, and his ring glinted, catching Jade's eye.

"Where are the other members of your cult who breezed into town a couple of days ago?" Jade asked the reverend.

"I have no idea what you're talking about."

"Huh?" Jade lifted her hand, and his wife gripped her throat as she was lifted off the ground. "I don't want to hurt your family," Jade told the reverend. "I like your wife and kids. They're good people." She looked at the reverend's wife. "I'm sorry, Marjorie."

"Let my wife go!" The reverend's voice boomed through the hall. "I had nothing to do with you being abducted or landing in the hands of Caleb and Kendal!"

Jade let Marjorie go. Her head snapped back to look at the reverend. "How do you know about those vile people?"

"It was on the news how a witch breezed through their garage and destroyed the place," the reverend told Jade.

"I never saw that on the news." Marjorie frowned. "I watch the news all the time."

"You must've missed it!" the Reverend snapped at his wife impatiently before turning back toward Jade. "I have held up my end of the accords all these years. You're the one breaking them."

"No..." Jade shook her head. "The minute you let your cult back into this town, you broke them."

"Jade..." the Reverend tried to reason with her, "remember the last time you went berserk what happened?" He swallowed again. "Please calm down."

"You're right." Jade breathed, and the powerful force swirling around her died down. "I'm sorry I scared your family."

"Go," Reverend Fletcher said to his wife and children. "Now!" he commanded.

His children ran off, but Marjorie stood staring at him.

"Go, woman!" The reverend glared at his wife.

"What have you done?" Marjorie shook her head at the reverend before giving Jade an apologetic look and walked from the room after her kids.

"I've lived by the accords for years." Jade followed the reverend into his living room.

"I know." The reverend walked over to a long cupboard and opened it.

"Then remember that," Jade said to the reverend's back. "Remember that I've lived like a dog chained in a garden and have never complained or rocked the boat. Even when my kind, including my daughter and myself, were victimized...." Her voice rose. "Victimized in our own town—a town we let your kind into when they needed a place to flee from the horrors of their own kind hundreds of years ago."

"What are you saying, Jade?" The reverend turned slightly from what he was doing in the cabinet to look at her.

"I don't need the town anymore, Reverend." Jade's eyes glowed violet once again. "My ancestors no longer linger here."

"What?" The reverend's eyes filled with fear.

Jade gave him a slow smile before she turned to leave. She knew what he was doing when his back was turned to her. As she walked away, she heard him cock the shotgun. She knew without turning around what the reverend held in his hand.

"I've been waiting for this day to come for a very long time." The reverend pulled the trigger.

Jade felt the pain burn like fire through her chest as she fell to the ground. Gripping her chest, Jade managed to turn onto her back. The reverend loomed over her, pointing the barrel of the shotgun at her face.

"No being should have that kind of power." The reverend cocked the gun again. "Especially not a woman." He gave a brittle laugh. "I want to say this gives me no pleasure, as you were the one to break the accords, but I'm actually so glad that you did."

His finger slipped onto the trigger.

"Now, I'm no longer obliged or under oath to protect you," the revered sneered. "A duty that made me sick to my stomach each day. You have just declared open season on magical beings once again." His finger inched closer to the trigger. "I wish I could make you watch as we obliterate the likes of you from this world, but I can't risk that." He went to pull the trigger, but it was jammed.

The reverend's eyes flew to Jade, who was now smiling up at him, and the wound on her chest was no longer seeping blood. Her powers once again started to kick up a storm in his living room as it lifted Jade up to a standing position.

"You really do love to preach, don't you, old man." Jade's eyes narrowed, and a smile spread across her lips. "I never broke the laws your kind forced on me. You and your hillbillies did."

The reverend's face started to pale as he realized what Jade had meant about her ancestors no longer lingering around their town. Fear coursed through him as his hand started to turn the shotgun to position the barrel beneath his chin.

"You need to get that angle just right," Jade taunted the reverend as the barrel was set in place by the reverend's own hands.

"Jade," the reverend pleaded, "let us talk about this."

"It's not a nice feeling when someone takes over your free will, is it?" Jade's eyes were bright pools of violet. "Unlike you, I don't like anyone to suffer, even evil dogs like you and your kind."

The reverend's eyes were huge with fear as his finger pulled the trigger.

Jade closed her eyes as the shot ripped through his skull, and he fell to the floor. She could not let his wife or kids see this. She spelled the house to make it look like he hung himself after Jade had left because of his remorse for what he'd done to her kind. She also added that he hoped Marjorie and his kids would forgive him for the years of abuse he put them through. It had sickened Jade that her mother would have made a deal with such a monster.

Marjorie had become known as the clumsiest woman in

town with all her bruises and broken limbs. Then, she'd become the town pariah when she'd been accused of caning her children, even when the kids had sworn it was not their mother. No one saw any evil in Reverend Fletcher. Well, now his family was free of him. Even still, Jade had taken no pleasure in killing the man. But he would've hunted her down, and it had to be done.

"MAYA." Dave pushed the plate of food back toward the young girl. "You have to eat. You'll need your strength if you ever come up against the bad people who got your mom."

"Weren't you one of those bad people?" Maya flicked the plate off the table, and it crashed to the floor. "You were the last one she was seen with."

"Maya..." Dave sighed and started to pick up the broken plate when the news playing on the TV caught his eye.

Dave left the broken plate to turn up the news. A family of three, namely Caleb, Kendal, and their son Junior, had just survived a vicious attack from a woman who they swear was a witch.

Dave's face paled as he saw their gas station was out near the desert. His heart started pounding as his phone rang. It was his brother. Dave answered the phone.

"Hello?" Dave's hand shook.

"Is there nothing you can't fuck up?" his brother hissed through the phone. "You had one chance to kill that dirty whore of a witch."

"I thought I had killed her," Dave said defensively. "You said yourself that Lawrence witches are hard to kill."

"Yes," his brother spat through the line, "and now we've lost the element of surprise."

"What do you want me to do?" Dave turned and saw the horrified look on Maya's face.

"Get your useless ass back into town," his brother demanded. "We need backup to finish this bitch off once and for all and take back our world."

EIGHT

THE ENFORCEMENT OF THE PEACE
ACCORDS PART 1

2001

James pulled into town in the brand-new Jeep his father had just bought him. He was staying at his grandmother's house for the summer. His father grew up in the town, and James' family had spent nearly every summer here when he was younger. James wondered if any of the guys he'd befriended when he was here ten years ago remembered him. He knew all the local hangouts in town, so as soon as he'd settled at his late grandmother's house, he was going to find out if some of his old friends were still around.

It wasn't long until James found himself surrounded by a group of new cohorts and a few of his old buddies who were still living here. The town hadn't changed too much, although many of the shops and diners he'd remembered had been replaced by others. James' new buddies were eager to please him. He found that when you had money to flash around—and he did—your friends became really loyal. James was having a lot of fun with the guys, and one day, while they were at the new local diner where all the kids hung out, he spotted one of the most beautiful girls he'd ever seen.

"Who's that?" James asked when the couple walked into the diner.

"That's Jade Lawrence," James' buddy told him.

"She's stunning!" James' eyes narrowed as he eyed her while she and Shaun took a seat in a booth.

"Yes," another male said, "she is one of the town's beauties. I know the guy she's with."

"Are they serious, or do you think she'd be interested in a summer fling with a handsome, rich boy?" James laughed, trying to make a joke of his desire. The minute she'd walked into the diner, he knew she was different somehow.

"You don't mess with her," Shaun's friend told James. "According to her fella, Jade has a dark secret."

"Yeah, man," one of the other guys said. "She's a witch."

"Her boyfriend, Shaun, told us that she does these really cool magic tricks," another boy said. "But not like boring magician magic tricks—*real* magic tricks."

"Really..." James looked at Jade. A slow smile crossed his lips as he started to turn the signet ring on his finger. It was a ring that his father had recently passed down to him to carry on the family legacy. "Do you think she'll show us some of her tricks? I know I have a few tricks of my own I'd like to show her." They all laughed and agreed that they'd enjoy that.

"I know where they'll be later," the guy who knew Jade's boyfriend told James. "Maybe we could go and ask her when we're all not in such a crowded place."

"Oh?" James looked at his friend. "Where is that?"

"We have the moonlight grove," the guy explained to James. "We all take our girls to... you know? To smooch and get it on."

"So I take it it's a secluded place then?" James' interest grew as an idea formulated in his mind. His father would be proud and know he made the right choice giving him the family ring.

"Yeah," the guy said, laughing. "There are quite a few openings, like secluded picnic areas, so you can't see the other people who are doing their thing in the next spot."

"Well, let's do that tonight then and go get us a magic show." Excitement spread through James. He was looking forward to meeting Jade later that night.

"IT'S A BIT COLD TONIGHT," Jade said to Shaun. "Can we stay in the car tonight?" She shuddered. There was a strange vibe in the air.

"Of course." Shaun nodded. "I don't mind where we are, as long as I'm with you."

"I brought us some snacks and soda." Jade pointed to the basket on the back seat of Shaun's car.

"You're the best." Shaun pulled Jade to him for a long, ardent kiss.

"Actually..." Jade smiled at Shaun as she straddled him on the driver's seat. "My mother made the snacks, so they're actually edible." Jade laughed at her reference to her not being very good in the kitchen.

Shaun pushed the seat back so Jade wasn't stuck up against the steering wheel. Their lips met again, and soon the food was forgotten as their kiss turned passionate.

"Shaun," Jade sighed as Shaun's lips moved down her neck.

"We won't do anything you're not ready to." Shaun's voice was hoarse with desire as his hands found Jade's shirt band and slipped beneath it to feel her soft, warm skin. "You're so beautiful."

Without saying anything, Jade took his warm hand and moved it toward her young, pert breast.

"Are you sure?" Shaun swallowed and looked into her passion-filled eyes.

"Yes." Jade nodded as she slid down onto his hardness and crushed her lips to his. "I'm not ready for the real thing yet," she whispered, kissing and nipping at his ear, "but I like what we do."

"So do I," Shaun breathed. He, too, was not ready to take their longing to the next level, but touching each other as they did was enough for both of them.

"Can we get onto the back seat?" Jade asked. "I don't want to accidentally hit the horn and have it blaring through the forest."

"I was just thinking the same thing." Shaun grinned at her.

Jade rolled back onto the passenger seat and grabbed a soda for each of them.

"I think we need one of these to cool off a little." Jade smiled at Shaun.

"Thank you." Shaun took the soda and popped the lid, and then had to swing his car door open as the soda fizzed up out of the can. "Shit, the can must've been shaken up in the back seat."

"Oh, no." Jade knelt over the seat and pulled some napkins from the basket. "Here." She handed them to Shaun.

Shaun had just finished cleaning up the soda when raucous shouts from a group of guys could be heard from behind the car. As Shaun turned to look, a few of the young men banged on the trunk, and cat called before shaking the car.

"Hey, Shaun." One guy appeared at the driver's window. "Come out and play!"

"Yeah!" another guy shouted. "Let's see some of your pretty lady's magic tricks."

"You told them?" Jade looked at Shaun in surprise. "I asked you not to say anything."

"I'm sorry, Babe." Shaun turned to Jade. "Some of the guys were bragging about their great girlfriends at football practice, and it just slipped out because I think you're the most amazing girl in town." He smiled at her apologetically.

"Shaun, you know I'm not allowed to show off my magic." Jade looked at him, not falling for the puppy dog's eyes routine. This was serious, and her mom would stop her from seeing Shaun if she knew. "You know that I've just turned sixteen, and this is the year I start to manifest my true powers at any moment, and a simple trick could turn dangerous."

"Come on, little witch," another one of the guys called. "Show us what you got."

"Show us a magic trick," another guy called from the other side of the car. They were surrounded.

"I know." Shaun held up his hands. "Can you just show them a few simple spells, and then they'll go away. They're just idiots who probably got into Simon's dad's liquor cabinet again."

"Fine," Jade hissed. "But after I've done a few spells, I want to go home," she growled.

"Jade, don't be like this." Shaun looked stricken. "It's still early, and I thought we could finish what we started." He leaned in to kiss her, but she pulled away.

"I think the mood's gone." Jade glared at him. "I'll get

my stuff ready." She reached over to the back and got her purse.

"Fine." Shaun sighed and got out of the car to deal with his idiotic friends.

"Get him," James ordered a few of the boys.

"What are you doing?" Shaun frowned as two of the boys grabbed and restrained him.

"Shaun?" Jade leaned toward the driver's side in alarm.

Jade witnessed him being restrained with both arms pressed behind his back as they leaned Shaun over the hood of the car. Before Jade could react, the passenger door flew open, and another large teenager she knew to be a year older than her grabbed her by the arm and dragged her out of the car.

"What are you doing?" Jade pulled her arm out of the guy's grip.

"Hello, Jade," James stepped into her view. "You really are beautiful." He gave her a smile. "I'm James, and my friends here have told me so much about you and your magic."

"Don't believe everything you hear!" Shaun shouted at James. "I was just messing with my friends when they were bragging about their cheerleader girlfriends." He struggled against the two large teenagers holding him down, but they twisted his arm painfully.

"Let Shaun go!" Jade ignored James and ran toward where the brutes held Shaun.

"If we do, will you show us some of your tricks?" James indicated to the guys holding Shaun to let him go.

Shaun pushed the guys away and ran around the car to Jade.

"She doesn't know magic," Shaun hissed at James. "Who the hell are you?"

"I'm here for the summer with my family," James told Shaun but never took his eyes off Jade. "I think we met when I was here visiting my grandmother ten years ago."

"I think I would've remembered meeting a shithead like you." Shaun grabbed Jade and pulled her protectively toward him. "Just go and leave us. Jade has to get home."

Shaun turned to open the passenger door while shielding Jade with his body, but some of James' new loyal friends grabbed Shaun and pulled him away from her. He turned and swung at one of them, only to get punched by another. Not liking being hit in the face by Shaun, the guy he'd managed to punch returned the favor before a bigger fight could break out, and James ordered them to stop fighting.

"We'll let you both go once we've seen a few tricks." James stepped up to Jade and cupped her chin with his hands. "I'd hate to see this beautiful face look sad if I let my friends beat up your boyfriend."

"Fine." Jade looked toward Shaun, who was struggling to break free of the two thugs holding him.

Jade could feel the anger boiling in the pit of her stomach. They were outnumbered as eight large teenage boys surrounded them. As she reached for her purse, her eyes fell on the ring James was twirling around his finger. She couldn't see what the top of the ring looked like as it was facing his palm, but she noted that he kept stroking and playing with it. It was like he was drawing his emotions from it, and Jade was sure she'd seen at least three flashes through his eyes in the past few minutes.

Jade performed a few simple harmless magic tricks for James and his teenage gang. They all stood watching in amazement as Jade used the various herbs and powders in her purse.

"There." Jade looked at James when she'd done her final trick. "That's all I know." She shoved the powder she'd used for her last exhibition into her purse. "Now, please go."

"Oh no, Jade." James stepped forward, blocking her path. "Your performance is not quite over for the night."

"James..." One of the teenagers who was with him didn't like the way things were going. "We've seen what we came here to see. I think we should go." He stepped up to James and tried to pull him away from Jade, but James sent him flying.

"Not yet," James hissed and stepped up to Jade. "We're going to have a bit of fun." He grabbed Jade by the hair, yanked her head back, and pressed her against the car. "Aren't we, Sweetheart?"

"Get off me." Jade shoved back, her eyes watering as his hand wrapped tighter in her hair.

"You little bitch." James slapped her across the face.

"Stop it!" Shaun struggled against the guys holding him. "Let her go or so help me—"

"Shut up." James' eyes were dark with excitement and lust. "Why don't you just relax and watch how a real man gets what he wants from a woman."

"Let her go!" Shaun struggled and managed to break one arm free, but he was quickly caught again and restrained. "You guys are dead!" he growled.

"Let me go!" Jade hissed, trying to slide her hand into her purse.

"Oh no, you don't!" James' face was very close to hers. "I'll take that." He pulled her purse off her arm and threw it out of her reach. "Now, where were we?"

James yanked Jade's hair, forcing her face up as he pressed his body against hers, brutally slamming her into the car.

"Do you feel how hard I am?" he said into her ear.

"Get off me!" Jade hissed again, her stomach churning and fear building up inside her.

She tried to push him off, but his hand left her hair, grabbed her wrists, and pulled her hands above her head. He held them up, forcing them painfully against the cold metal of the car.

"Let's see what's beneath this shirt," James whispered.

"James..." The guy he'd pushed away ran at him again. "That's enough!"

"Fuck off!" James grabbed Jade and threw her on the ground before turning on the guy and drawing out a knife. "I will use this on you if you come near me again." He turned to look at the rest of his new gang, who stood staring at him, stunned. "That goes for all of you."

While James was threatening his crew, Jade scrambled to get up, only to have James kick her back down with a boot to her chest.

"Where do you think you're going, little witch?" James smiled evilly down at her. "You still have to satisfy me." He raised his knife and then dropped down to his knees, straddling her. "To bed a witch..." He ran the knife down from her throat and between her breasts all the way down to the top button of her jeans.

"Please..." Tears were now running down Jade's eyes. "Get off me."

"Oh, come now. You know you want this." James grabbed the crotch of his jeans. The outline of his arousal pushed against them as he slipped his hands under the band of her jeans. "Mmm, what have we here?"

"Stop it, please." Jade tried to grab his hand as it painfully pressed into a place not even her boyfriend's hand had been.

James laughed, pulled his hand from her jeans, grabbed her shirt, and was about to cut through it when his gang of new friends yelled at him to stop. Before he turned to them to tell them to go to hell, Shaun broke free and tackled James. The knife went flying as James and Shaun started to scuffle.

James managed to overpower Shaun, but when he stood to turn back to Jade, he stopped. His eyes grew wide as he saw Jade was now wielding the knife. Her face was bruised from where he'd hit her, and her lip was bleeding from the second slap he'd given her. Her clothes were stained with dirt, and her cheeks wet with tears.

NINE

THE ENFORCEMENT OF THE PEACE ACCORDS PART 2

2001, continued

In their car's headlights, James saw Jade's eyes turn violet, and her hair billowed out as she stood chanting. She held up her palm and sliced through her soft flesh with the knife, drawing blood. With the knife in one hand and blood seeping from her other hand, Jade dripped blood onto the earth. A wind of magical energy started to swirl around her as a gold light exploded around them.

The gang of teenagers, including James, covered their eyes with their arms. When the light cleared, Jade's powers had been completely unlocked, and the blood that had dripped on the earth below her called to her ancestors. The moon's light was dim as dark clouds blocked it, and the heavens above started to rumble angrily. Lightning split through the sky as the magical wind that had surrounded Jade picked up into gale-force winds that bent the trees around them.

"Jade…" James held up his hands in front of him. "Stop these parlor tricks." He screamed at her, knowing full well they weren't parlor tricks but powerful magic.

Jade let go of the knife, and it floated up next to her as she stalked toward James. He tried to step away, but he couldn't move. A magical force held him to the ground.

"It doesn't feel good to be held by force, does it?" Jade stepped up to James. Her violet eyes were blank and emotionless. "Let me show you how a real witch treats bullies and rapists."

Jade flicked her hand, James' legs buckled and he fell to the ground. With her bloody hand, Jade twisted the hand he'd brutally shoved down her pants and telekinetically broke every finger on that hand before cracking his wrist.

James screamed in pain. When he tried to grab his wrist with the other hand, Jade broke that hand too, as it was the one he'd slapped her with.

"You will never attack another woman, no matter who she is!" Jade's eyes looked coldly down at him. "Ever again."

With a twist of her wrist, James's body started to contort awkwardly. His screams of pain were blanked out by the storm raging all around them. Not wanting to stick around, James' gang tried to take off in James' car, but it wouldn't start, and when they looked up at the dashboard, Jade was standing there staring at them. She raised her hands, but before she sent the car flying, most of the boys jumped out and started fleeing through the woods.

Anger had taken control of Jade's senses. She walked up to where Shaun still lay on the ground, unconscious. She knew he was still alive and sacrificed a few drops of her blood on his right side, left side, above his head and below his feet in order to protect him from the magical storm raging within her.

As the storm gathered power around her, parts of trees were blown loose and sent flying in all directions. At the same time, the earth opened a path through the woods for

Jade, pointing her in the direction in which the rest of James' gang had run. Ignoring James' agonizing cries as he lay broken on the ground, Jade started after the boys who had done nothing to help her.

Jade slowed a few of the boys down with her magic, sending them flying and cracking against the trees like bugs hitting a windshield. Every time she knocked one of the boys down, a flash of lightning split the sky and shot to the earth. One of the lightning forks hit a tree and ricocheted onto two others. The trees went up in flames, and as Jade pursued the last few boys as they ran out of the woods and into the town, the forest started to burn.

Jade cleared the woods in pursuit of the last few boys who had laughed and cheered James on. She didn't care that they'd tried to stop him at the last minute. It should never have gotten as far as it had in the first place. It was those boys who had blabbed about her to that psycho and brought him to her and Shaun's favorite spot. They were responsible for Shaun being unconscious and her being assaulted. She was tired of being treated differently and tired of men leering at her suggestively and thinking they could take whatever they wanted.

As Jade walked through the streets, scattered debris flew, and the wind swirled behind her as the storm followed her, causing chaos in the small town. She hardly heard the screams or the sounds of the police, ambulance, and fire truck sirens as she followed the magical path to her next victim.

GRACE LAWRENCE HEARD the screams coming from the woods echo through her head as the earth called her for help. She closed her eyes and saw the flames engulfing the forest, swiftly following the forceful winds toward the town. Grace also knew the storm moving in over the town was not a natural storm. She tried to conjure up the witch who had brought them about, but she ran into a magical wall.

Grace's eyes flew open in fear. She knew all the witches, both male and female, in town. None of those witches were this powerful. In fact, there were only two families of witches who could conjure such power. A chill crept up her spine, but before she could ponder on the source of the magical storm, pictures of firefighters struggling to put out the blaze flashed through her mind. The fire was on the edge of the town.

Grace took out her dagger, sliced her palm, did an incantation, and was magically transported to the forest. She appeared next to the firefighters who were struggling to put out the angry fire that raged above them like a demon from Hell. She drew on all her powers and doused the flames. The firefighters looked at her, stunned and amazed, before grudgingly thanking her and taking off into the woods to look for victims who may have been caught in the blaze.

Grace traced the source of the fire back to one of what Grace liked to call the woods' picnic pods. What she found made her blood grow cold and confirmed her suspicions as to who the witch was who had drawn the magical storm.

"Shaun." Grace ran forward to where the young man was lying motionless on the ground.

Grace felt for a pulse, and it was still strong. She noted that he had been spelled, and so the area around him had been protected. Her eyes moved across the scene, and her horrified gaze fell upon another young man lying on the ground. His body was hideously contorted and it looked like every bone in his body had been broken.

"Jade," Grace whispered, "what have you done?"

Grace went over to the boy and felt for a pulse. The moment she touched him, scenes from the night unfolded in her brain. She pulled away from him as if she'd been burned. Grace had to swallow down her anger and a desire to crush him more. When she bent to scoop up Jade's purse, the ground beneath her rumbled in warning, and another vision crossed her mind. Jade had not yet finished her mission, and only Grace had the power to stop her.

She called to the firefighters that she'd found two young men and left them in the firefighters' care as she disappeared to go find her daughter before she burned down the town. There were some things you never recovered from. Grace knew that once the anger faded from her daughter, the remorse of how she retaliated could only have two outcomes, both of which Grace would rather avoid having her daughter suffer.

GRACE FOUND Jade standing in the middle of the town's main street. She struggled to get near her daughter as the storm that protected Jade tried to keep her away. Jade stood with a dagger in one hand, carving symbols on the arm of her blood-stained hand. In front of Jade were three teenage boys she knew must've been part of the crowd she'd seen in her vision.

"Jade!" Grace shouted through the storm to her daughter, but Jade ignored her.

Grace knew the only way she could calm Jade down was to draw the storm into herself. She ran over to one of the bystanders cowering on the side of the road. She knew always carried a pocketknife and asked to borrow it. She told him if he didn't want to see his son—one of the boys kneeling in front of Jade—writhe in pain at any minute, to give it to her.

The man nodded and handed it to Grace. She walked into the storm and grounded herself as the wind brutally tried to whip her back. Grace drew the blade across her soft flesh and started her incantations. As she dropped her blood onto the earth, she knew it was going to be a fierce battle. As she soaked up the power, she started to feel sick, as if her insides were going to burst. Never before had she felt such a force, but she held her ground until she'd funneled the power away. As the wind dropped and the black storm clouds disappeared, Grace fell to the ground and was horribly sick. As she vomited the darkness from her soul, she fought to stay conscious and not let it overwhelm her.

Her head ached, and her ears rang. She barely heard the angry shouts of the townspeople as she pushed herself to her feet. Grace turned to see the angry mob circling her and Jade. They poured out of their houses, shops, and establishments, shouting about the accords that bound this town to live in peace and brought the witch trials to an end all those centuries ago. They shouted that for this, Jade should burn like her ancestors did. They demanded retribution. Jade must be punished.

"It was them who attacked me!" Jade's voice boomed, sending a pulse through the angry mob, forcing them backward. "Why don't you ask them what they did to me?" She screamed at the top of her voice. "You all shout about us living in peace with you!" She carried on screaming "Yet none of you live in peace with us. This is MY TOWN!"

The wind started to pick up around Jade again.

"Do you hear me?" Dark clouds started to roll from above, and the ground rumbled with the force of the storm rolling in once again.

Grace had to summon all her power as she saw the runes carved into Jade's forearms start to glow. Her blood once again went cold, and her breath caught in her throat as she recognized those runic symbols. Not a witch in her family line, or any other, had seen them in over two thousand years. Grace knew that, even if it killed her, if she didn't contain Jade right at that moment, her daughter would come into full power all at once. There was a reason why up until the age of sixteen witches could only use soft magic, which was fundamental healing spells and parlor tricks. From sixteen, their powers were gradually unlocked as they grew and learned from their elders how to control and focus their magic.

Witches whose magic-filled them all at once either went mad or were drawn to the darker side of magic. With Jade's kind of power, that Grace now knew she had, an angry and dark Jade would destroy everything in her path, and there would be no stopping her. Jade was drawing from an ancient power that had been simmering and absorbing energies from generations of witches who'd long since left this realm.

"Jade!" Grace screamed at her daughter. "Stop this!" She squeezed her palm, reopening the wound, and let her blood drip on the earth as she rushed to her daughter's side.

Grace wrapped Jade in her arms and ran her bloody palm over Jade's symbols carved into her flesh. Within seconds, she felt her daughter relax against her. The storm instantly stopped, and Jade went limp for a second, nearly knocking Grace to the ground.

The townspeople surrounded them and demanded that

Jade be punished. To stop them from hurting Jade and save them from themselves, Grace came to an arrangement with them. Grace knew that what Jade had awakened would destroy this town and everyone in it if Jade was harmed. The accords were rewritten and included that Jade's powers were bound. She could still do her herbs and potions, and Grace would have to leave town. Too much power in one place. Jade went to live with Suzie and her father, as the townspeople didn't know about Suzie—Grace had made sure of that.

That was the last day Grace had seen her daughter, but she knew she'd see her again when the time came. The power that flowed through Jade was not a power that could be contained for too long.

TEN

TO KILL A LAWRENCE WITCH

Two Days Ago

"Hi," Jade answered her front door to find Dave standing there.

"Hi." Dave smiled down at Jade. "Sorry to drop by unannounced."

"It's fine." Jade grinned up at him. They'd been sneaking around for the past two nights. "Do you want to come in? Maya isn't home." She gave him a slow smile. "She's out for the whole afternoon."

"I'd love to..." Dave cleared his throat. "But I've got some business to attend to."

"Pity." Jade smiled.

"I know you spoke about your mother, Grace Lawrence, the other night and how you wondered where she was," Dave said. "I found this." He handed her a pamphlet.

The pamphlet advertised Amazing Grace, a magical and minstrel traveling show. It promised that you'd be wowed by the magic, have your fortune told, and could buy some of their amazing herbs and healing oils.

"I've seen this show. They pass through a nearby town

once a year." Jade shrugged and frowned as Dave scrolled through his phone. "It doesn't mean this is my mother, just because the show running is called Amazing Grace."

"The website advertises her name as Grace Lawrence." Dave turned his phone toward Jade. "They'll be in the next town the day after tomorrow. I thought you and I could go check it out on an official date." He gave her a boyish grin.

That weird feeling that had not left her alone for days now gripped her spine once again, and the flesh on her left forearm started to burn. She swallowed and casually rubbed the skin on her aching arm.

"Are you okay?" Dave looked down at where Jade was rubbing her arm.

"I'm fine." Jade fobbed off his concern. "Just a little allergy. It's the wool of my jersey," she lied to him.

"So?" Dave looked at her hopefully. "Can I pick you up the day after tomorrow at about ten in the morning to go on a short road trip to see Amazing Grace?"

"Sure." Jade nodded. "Why not."

"Great." Dave pulled Jade toward him and crushed his lips to hers in a passionate kiss. Their bodies instantly responded to each other, but Dave knew he had to go, so he pushed her away and cleared his throat. "I'll see you then."

"Okay," Jade said in a bit of a daze after the kiss—a kiss in which she'd tasted uncertainty, longing, a little bit of guilt, and perhaps sorrow. Her brows drew together as she watched Dave drive off. The creepy cold feeling gained intensity, and her arm stung.

Jade pulled back her sleeve to see the faint lines of the runes she once carved into her arms turn pink. Something was up, but she couldn't quite put a finger on it. She shook the feeling off and went back to her workshop.

Yesterday

Dave and Jade dropped Maya off at Suzie's house. They were going to stay over in the next town for the night, so Suzie was having Maya stay with her.

The drive to the next town was only an hour, and Jade was looking forward to the drive with Dave even though her arm was burning and itching like crazy. She'd put some cream on it, but it hardly soothed the scars.

Jade and Dave hadn't been driving for more than thirty minutes when a marquee tent could be seen off to one side of the road. Dave pulled up to the tent.

"This is not what I pictured the show to be." Jade looked at Dave questioningly. "I thought there'd be more cars, more shows, and at least some signs."

Her arm was aching like mad, but Jade ignored it. She didn't like this part of town. It was near the desert, and unless she was with someone she thoroughly trusted, it creeped her out. It suddenly dawned on her. It was Dave who gave her this creepy, unsettled feeling.

"It's probably to create some sort of weird eerie atmosphere." Dave shrugged. "I say we at least go in and take a look. We're here now."

"Sure." Jade climbed out of the car and grabbed her purse, hugging it close to her.

Dave led the way as he disappeared into the tent. Jade had the sudden urge to turn and run. Something wasn't right here. Before she could make a move, Dave reappeared, grabbed her wrist, and yanked her into the tent.

"Hello, Jade." A scarred man in a wheelchair rolled up in front of her. "Remember me?"

"You!" Jade's stomach churned, and a fire started to spark in her stomach. She turned to run, but three large men stepped in her way, and Dave once again latched onto her wrist.

"I see you do remember me, as you're the one who did this to me." James indicated the chair and his scars. "Condemned me to a wheelchair and a life of daily excruciating pain. The doctors asked me if I'd fallen from a tall building and been dumped in the woods. That's how badly broken and twisted my bones were, Witch."

"Get her bag," Dave told one of the henchmen.

"This is your big brother," Jade's eyes filled with anger, hurt, betrayal, and disgust as she glared at Dave, suddenly recognized the ring.

"Yes." Dave looked like he was torn between his loyalty to his brother and his growing feelings for Jade.

"His exploits are what you thought you'd never live up to?" Jade hissed at Dave in disgust. "Do you even know what his exploits were?"

"My brother was ridding this world of creatures like you, as did my father before him, and a long line of my ancestors." Dave swallowed and kept his feelings hidden.

"You mean they murdered magical beings and stole their world from them," Jade corrected him.

"I've never been so proud of my little bro." James leered at Jade. "He got to do what I couldn't." He looked up at Dave with an evil smile. "He managed to bed a witch, and not just any witch, a *Lawrence* witch." He looked at Jade with blatant hate.

"Well, you certainly couldn't get it up anymore." Jade gave him a snide smile. "That was something I made sure no one would ever fix for you."

"You little bitch." James indicated for his goons to get Jade to kneel in front of him. He grabbed her hair while his goons pinned her hands painfully at her back. "I can still feel some sensation there. Do you want to try and see if you can bring it back to life?" He was about to stuff her face into his groin when Dave intervened.

"James," Dave said warningly. "I personally don't want to see you get off with anyone, and I'm sure no one else here does either."

James yanked Jade's hair, pulling her head back, and then punched her in the face with his other hand before pushing her away.

"Let's see how you feel receiving a near-death beating." James nodded to his guards, who dragged Jade to one side and started to strike her.

Pain echoed through every inch of Jade's flesh as two men held her up while another used her as a punching bag.

"That's enough!" Dave stopped the men. "This isn't part of the plan. You wanted her dead, not beaten to a pulp. How are you going to take a photograph of her to prove she's dead with her face swollen beyond recognition?"

"Fine..." James stopped his men. "But I've decided I want her shot and left to bleed out in the desert where wild animals will feast on her flesh while she's still just alive enough to feel it." His eyes filled with malice.

"Okay." Dave agreed with James. "But you said as I bedded her, I get to kill her."

"Of course." James smiled. "Now take the bitch away and finish her off as I told you to."

Dave nodded, grabbed Jade, and started to drag her out of the tent, taking her purse with them.

"I don't need an audience for the ritual of bedding and then slaying," Dave told his brother. "We need to dump this in the desert, so no one traces this back to us except the society."

Dave shoved Jade in the car. She was barely conscious after the beating James' goons had given her. He drove them into the middle of the desert. He knew that his brother's goons would follow them, and he hated what he had to do.

In a secluded spot in the desert, Dave pulled Jade from the car and pushed her onto the ground. He pulled his gun out of the glove compartment and then loomed over her before straddling her.

"I have to make it look like I'm having sex with you," Dave told her. "It is part of the society's ritual to bed a witch and then kill them," he explained to an almost unconscious Jade. "I can't bear to rape any woman, even a witch. I enjoyed meeting you, and I half fell in love with you. You were nothing like my brother said you were."

Dave pretended to collapse upon Jade after finishing the bedding part of the ritual.

"If you were anyone else, I would've fallen in love with you." Dave pulled her face toward himself and gave her one last kiss. "I'm nothing like them. This ritual makes me sick to my stomach, but you're my way out of this life. I am sorry. Goodbye, Jade." He knocked her out with the handle of the gun. He stood up and pretended to pull up his pants.

Dave aimed the gun at her head, but he couldn't bring himself to kill her. He fired two shots into the sand next to her head, took a picture of her lifeless body, and then left her in the desert as he pulled away. He drove a few yards, emptying the contents of her purse as he went, before dumping her empty purse. Dave had already rifled through Jade's wallet and had taken out the picture of Maya.

ELEVEN

A NEW PEACE IN AN OLD TOWN

Present Day

Jade burst into the house of a man by the name of Nigel. Items flew as she walked, and the closer she got to Nigel, the deeper the runes on her arm got. When Nigel saw her, his eyes grew large with terror as memories of another night that Jade had come after him flashed through his mind. Nigel had been filled with anger and fear when he'd reported her to the Reverend Fletcher a week or so ago for scaring his boy with her magic. He'd done that when he still thought the accords were in place. He now knew the reverend was dead and had heard the rumors and seen the news.

"Hello, Nigel." Jade's eyes were glowing violet pools. "Where is your buddy James hiding out?"

"Jade..." Nigel tried to calm her down. He knew the only reason she'd spared his life that day was because he kept trying to pull James off of her. "I don't know. I've not seen or heard from him in years. I don't agree with him or his weird secret society."

"Come now, Nigel." Jade raised an eyebrow. "You know I can spot a lie from miles away."

"If I tell you, will you leave my family alone?" Nigel looked at her with fear in his eyes, but something in him shifted. Something about her made him realize she would not harm him. "I can find out for you," he said softly.

"You're a decent guy, Nigel." Jade calmed down. "You need to teach your son some manners, but otherwise, you and your wife have always been kind."

"That man is at his grandmother's old house on the outskirts of town." Molly, Nigel's wife, popped out of the kitchen. "Nigel is telling the truth, Jade. That man came here and tried to stir up trouble, but Nigel kicked him out."

"Thank you, Molly." Jade clicked her fingers and cleaned up the mess she'd caused.

"Can you teach me that trick?" Molly looked at her, amazed, but her smile was wiped off her face when a rumbling commotion was heard.

"Dad?" Nigel's son ran downstairs, stopping when he saw Jade. "Trucks and army-looking guys are coming down the main street."

"Stay here," Jade told them.

"You can't go out there alone," Molly told her.

"Please. I don't want anyone else getting hurt." Jade gave them a sad smile. "They have Maya and left me to die in the desert. This is my fight." She nodded and walked out onto their porch and pulled the door closed telekinetically.

Two big trucks carrying men dressed in a secret society uniform rolled down the road. James was driven in a convertible by Dave. At the same time, he cited bible passages through a bullhorn in between, telling the townspeople to give up the witches, especially Jade.

Jade closed her eyes and let her mind travel up the road.

She froze when she saw Maya tied up in the trunk of the convertible. Her eyes flew open, and her arm was on fire. She turned her arm and saw the red, angry scars of the runes. She looked around the porch for something sharp.

"You're going to need this." Nigel handed her the dagger James had used all those years ago. "I'm sorry, Jade. I know you told me not to interfere, but this is also our fight. My great, great, going back years, great grandfather's father was one of the missionaries your ancestors helped." He cocked the shotgun he held in his arms. "We just want to live in peace with each other. We need your kind and respect that you let us live here."

"You should be the mayor." Jade gave Nigel a tight smile.

"That's what I keep saying!" Molly stepped out and cocked her handgun. "We're not the only ones behind you, Jade. We were all just shit-scared of that tyrant, Reverend Fletcher."

"Even his wife and children were scared of him," Nigel told her.

"If it weren't for you..." Marjorie stepped onto the porch, surprising Jade. "I would be covering up more bruises."

"Thank you." Tears misted Jade's eyes. "Stay back until I've neutralized the situation."

Jade swallowed and gritted her teeth as she took the dagger and reopened the runes on her arm. She sliced her palm again and let the blood drop onto their porch. She stepped into the middle of the road as the trucks turned the corner and started to make their way past Nigel's house.

"There she is!" James pointed at her, screaming wildly.

By the time they got close to Jade, her magic was back to full force and more powerful than all those years ago. Only now, Jade had more control. James grabbed Dave's pistol, but before he could fire it, his hand moved and aimed the barrel at his own head.

The townspeople had started to gather. Only this time, they weren't welding pitchforks or yelling for Jade to be punished; they were banding together to get the bad element out of town. They were tired of living in fear and feeling divided. As soon as the reverend had died, it was like a huge weight had been lifted from the town. No longer did they have to pick a side. They felt they could live side by side and get to know their neighbors instead of fearing them because of another person's prejudice or fears.

"What are you doing, James?" Dave slammed on the brakes.

The truck behind him nearly rammed the back of his car, but it was stopped. His head flew around to see Jade's eyes trained on James. Her left arm was bleeding, as was her palm. Her hair billowed out while wind swirled around her.

"James!" Dave reached up to try to pull his brother's hand away from pointing the gun at his own head, but he couldn't move it. It was like his arm had frozen into position. "Please, Jade! Don't do this." His eyes were filled with fear.

James' soldiers jumped out of the truck and aimed their weapons at her. Still, they flew out of the soldier's hands, and they were forced to their knees by the other witches of the town while the townspeople jumped in and rounded them all up.

"Tell him to confess what he did, not only to me but all those women he hurt," Jade hissed.

The bullhorn was back in James' hand and raised to his lips.

"Confess!" Jade shouted, and the townspeople banded around her.

"Don't you see what she's doing to you?" James shouted through the bullhorn. "They are evil, and you will all burn in Hell for siding with these demons!" he screamed, his face turning red with hate.

"Confess, confess, confess..." the people of the town started chanting.

While their attention was drawn away from the trunk, Jade telekinetically linked with Ethan. The latter magically appeared at the back of Dave's convertible and snuck Maya out of the trunk and to safety.

Once Maya was safe, Jade climbed into James' mind and made him tell the whole town what he used to do to both normal girls and witches alike. He admitted what he'd planned to do with Jade and what he had done to her to the entire town, including his brother, who went pale as he listened. Dave's eyes turned to meet Jade's. Remorse, regret, and defeat shone in his eyes.

Jade released James from the mental link she had on him. His hands dropped to his side, but he quickly lifted the gun and took aim at Jade, but before he could pull the trigger, Dave dived on him. The gun went off, and James slumped in his seat, dead.

Dave and the rest of the secret society soldiers were rounded up and handed over to the FBI, who'd been tracking them for a long time. They were going to rot in federal prison.

Dave asked to see Jade, and when she went to him, he gave her back the picture of Maya. He told her that he was sorry. Jade didn't say a word to him until she was about to leave.

"You're lucky the feds came when they did," Jade told Dave. "The town's people were looking forward to crucifying you naked on a flagpole as a warning to others like you."

MAYA WAS sad to leave her hometown behind, but Jade had promised her they'd be back. Jade had received a letter from Grace telling her how proud she was of what she'd achieved in their little town. There was actual peace, and the town would no longer stand for any discrimination of any kind. The people had started to talk to each other and not through some biased third party that held their power by keeping them segregated by fear and hate. At the end of the letter, Grace had said that what had happened all those years ago was never Jade's fault.

Maya and Jade were heading to another town that needed their help and where Maya had found out Grace's troop would be heading soon. She was finally going to meet her grandmother.

They stopped at a gas station to fill up. While Jade was filling up the car, Maya slipped into the shop to get snacks. As she was coming out of the shop, four teenage boys stood in her way, trying to get fresh with her and saying lewd things. Maya tried to step around them, but they wouldn't let her step past.

"See that woman over there?" Maya nodded toward her mother. "She's my mother and a witch."

"What is she going to do?" the one boy jeered. "Zap us?"

"No." Maya touched the boy's arm, and he buckled to the ground. "I'll zap you. My mother... well, she's a full-powered witch."

The boy's eyes grew huge as he looked toward Jade,

who was now frowning at the scene. Before Jade could walk over to her daughter, the boys took off.

"What was that all about?" Jade asked Maya taking the shopping bag from her.

"Nothing I couldn't handle." Maya shrugged.

"Okay..." Jade smiled. "Let's hit the road." She turned and walked back to the car.

Maya smiled as she levitated a piece of wood off the ground and sent it into the wall. She took a deep, satisfying breath as she no longer felt afraid or small. Her arm itched. She turned it around, and an ancient rune symbol appeared on her arm in the form of a pink birthmark.

ABOUT THE AUTHOR

Renee Joiner has been in love with the supernatural for longer than she can remember, so it is no surprise that she is an author of paranormal urban fantasy. Although she discovered her passion for writing when she was only twelve years old, she didn't make her writing debut until many years into the future. Adventurous and fun-loving, she enjoys traveling to new places, exploring new sights and meeting new people. Thus, she delights in creating fantastical worlds that are sure to give her readers an escape from the real world while simultaneously providing thrilling entertainment.

Besides her special knack for writing, you'll also find a passion for metaphysics spirituality which she has been nurturing for over four decades. Renee hails from New York and currently resides with her husband in their empty nest—unless you count their three adorable fur babies—in Florida. She enjoys adding to her sea of knowledge and thus spends her free time learning new things.

To find out more about Renee Joiner, feel free to visit her **official website**.

facebook.com/reneejoinerauthor

twitter.com/iamreneejoiner

instagram.com/reneejoinerauthor

amazon.com/author/reneejoiner

SERIES BY RENEE

Thorne Sisters Chronicles
Possessed by Magic
Reincarnated by Magic
Immortal by Magic

SIGN UP TO RECEIVE MY
NEWLETTER FOR ALL THE
LATEST UPDATES AND SPECIALS!

RENEEJOINERAUTHOR.COM/NEWSLETTER

Thank You...

Thank you for reading my book!
I really appreciate all of your feedback and I love to hear what you have to say. Please leave your review at your favorite retailer!

www.ingramcontent.com/pod-product-compliance
Lightning Source LLC
Chambersburg PA
CBHW022044170626
46808CB00003B/1362